ARI BERK

LOREN LONG

Simon & Schuster Books for Young Readers
New York   London   Toronto   Sydney   New Delhi

SIMON & SCHUSTER BOOKS FOR YOUNG READERS

An imprint of Simon & Schuster Children's Publishing Division · 1230 Avenue of the Americas, New York, New York 10020 · Text copyright © 2012 by Ari Berk · Illustrations copyright © 2012 by Loren Long · All rights reserved, including the right of reproduction in whole or in part in any form. · SIMON & SCHUSTER, Inc. · For information about special discounts for bulk purchases, please contact Simon & Schuster Special Sales at 1-866-506-1949 or business@simonandschuster.com. · The Simon & Schuster Speakers Bureau can bring authors to your live event. For more information or to book an event, contact the Simon & Schuster Speakers Bureau at 1-866-248-3049 or visit our website at www.simonspeakers.com. · Book design by Dan Potash · The text for this book is set in Caslon Manuscript. · The illustrations for this book are rendered in acrylic and graphite. · Manufactured in China · 0612 SCP · 10 9 8 7 6 5 4 3 2 1 · Library of Congress Cataloging-in-Publication Data · Berk, Ari. · Nightsong / Ari Berk ; illustrated by Loren Long. — 1st ed. p. cm. · Summary: Chiro, a young bat, is nervous about flying into the world for the first time without his mother, especially on a very dark night, but he soon learns to rely on his "song" to find his way and stay safe. · ISBN 978-1-4169-7886-2 (hardcover : alk. paper) — ISBN 978-1-4169-8552-5 (eBook) · 1. Bats—Juvenile fiction. [1. Bats—Fiction. 2. Echolocation (Physiology)—Fiction.] I. Long, Loren, ill. II. Title. · PZ10.3.B45236Nig 2012 · [E]—dc22 · 2009026608

first edition

For my mother and my son
—A. B.

To my father
—L. L.

The sun had set, and the shadows clinging to the walls of the cave began to wake and whisper.

"Chiro? Little Wing?" the bat-mother said to her child. "Tonight you must fly out into the world, and I will wait here for you."

"But the night is dark, Momma . . . darker than the moth's dark eyes . . . darker even than the water before dawn," the little bat exclaimed, twitching his ears this way and that.

"I know," whispered his mother.

"And when it is that dark outside, I cannot always see," Chiro admitted, stretching his wings.

"There are other ways to see," she told him, "other ways to help you make your way in the world."

"How?"

"Use your *good sense*."

"What is *sense*?" the little bat asked.

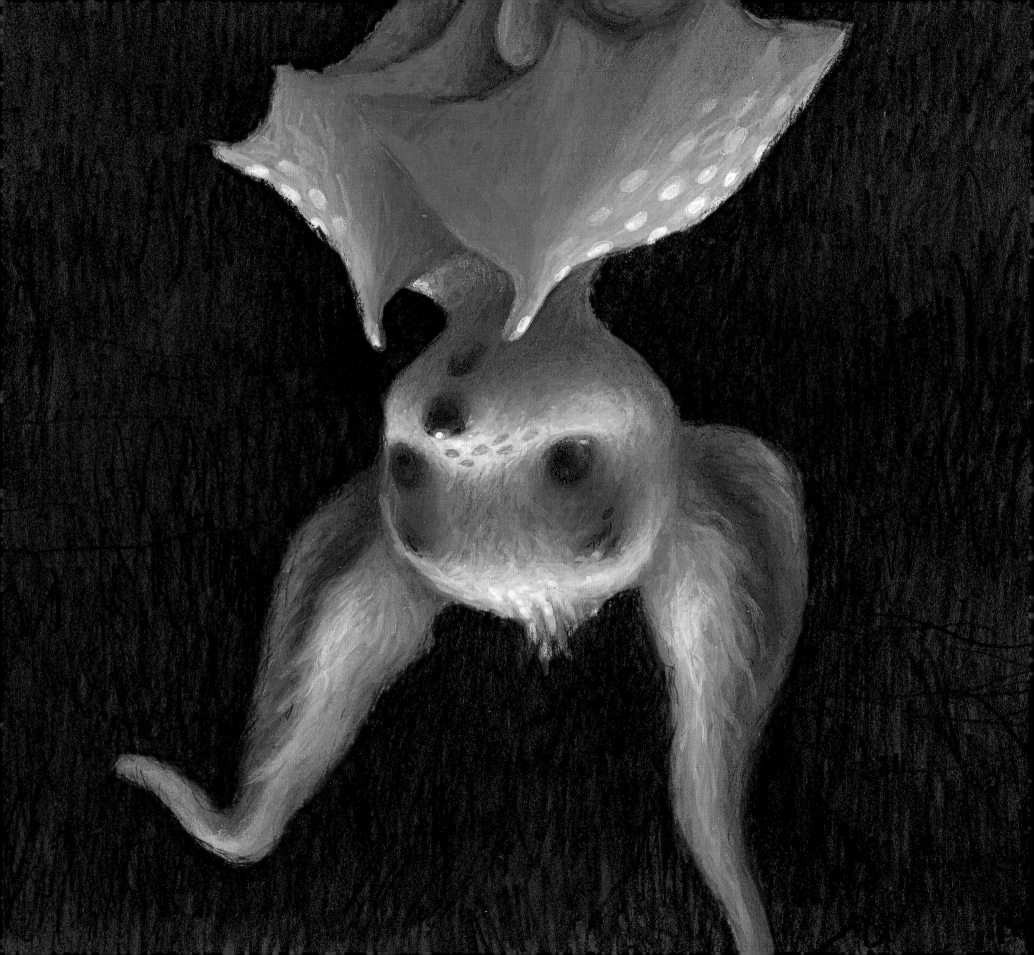

His mother folded him in her wings and whispered into his waiting ears, "*Sense* is the song you sing out into the world, and the song the world sings back to you. Sing, and the world will answer. That is how you'll see.

"Now fly from our cave to the pond where we bats like best to eat. Have your breakfast, then fly home, but do not go farther than the pond, not unless your song is sure."

And then she let him go.

Chiro fell into the cold air for an instant, then flapped and turned and flew out past the mouth of the cave and into the waiting night.

At first Chiro tried to peer his way through the dark. Long arms rose up in front of him, waving slowly, blocking his path. He could not see around them, or over them. Chiro was frightened.

But he remembered his mother's bright words:
"Use your *good sense.*"

Chiro began to sing. Softly at first . . .

. . . but then more surely. His song flew ahead of
him, and soon he could hear something singing back.

Tall trees called out to him, chanted the lengths
of their long branches and the girths of their rough
trunks. Gleefully, he flew through the woods, past
pines, over maples, and away.

Flying higher now, Chiro saw something sliding through
the sky toward him.

So out went his song, and where danger once threatened,
now Chiro saw only a flock of friends flying above him
on their evening errands.

As he flew farther, Chiro heard strange
sounds: lines of noise, a thousand voices
buzzing from one end of the sky to the
other. For just a moment, Chiro didn't
know what to do or which way to go.

But he followed his own song. In the
sky behind him flowed a river of
whispers, fading away. The pond was
just ahead.

When Chiro came to the pond, singing still, he was very hungry. All the night creatures were there above the reeds, thousands of tiny, flying tasty things, each one humming a different tune. For Chiro each of their songs sounded like breakfast.

Chiro ate well that night.

When he was full, he stretched his wings again and thought about flying home, but he began to wonder, just a little. What lay beyond the pond? What lay beyond his mother's words?

So Chiro flew a bit farther and the familiar
fell away from him. Out, out to the margins
of the world. Then he was truly on his own.

He flew fast toward a high dune, each grain of sand calling out in chorus as he passed. Chiro flapped up and over the top of the dune and out over the strand, singing louder than he ever sang before.

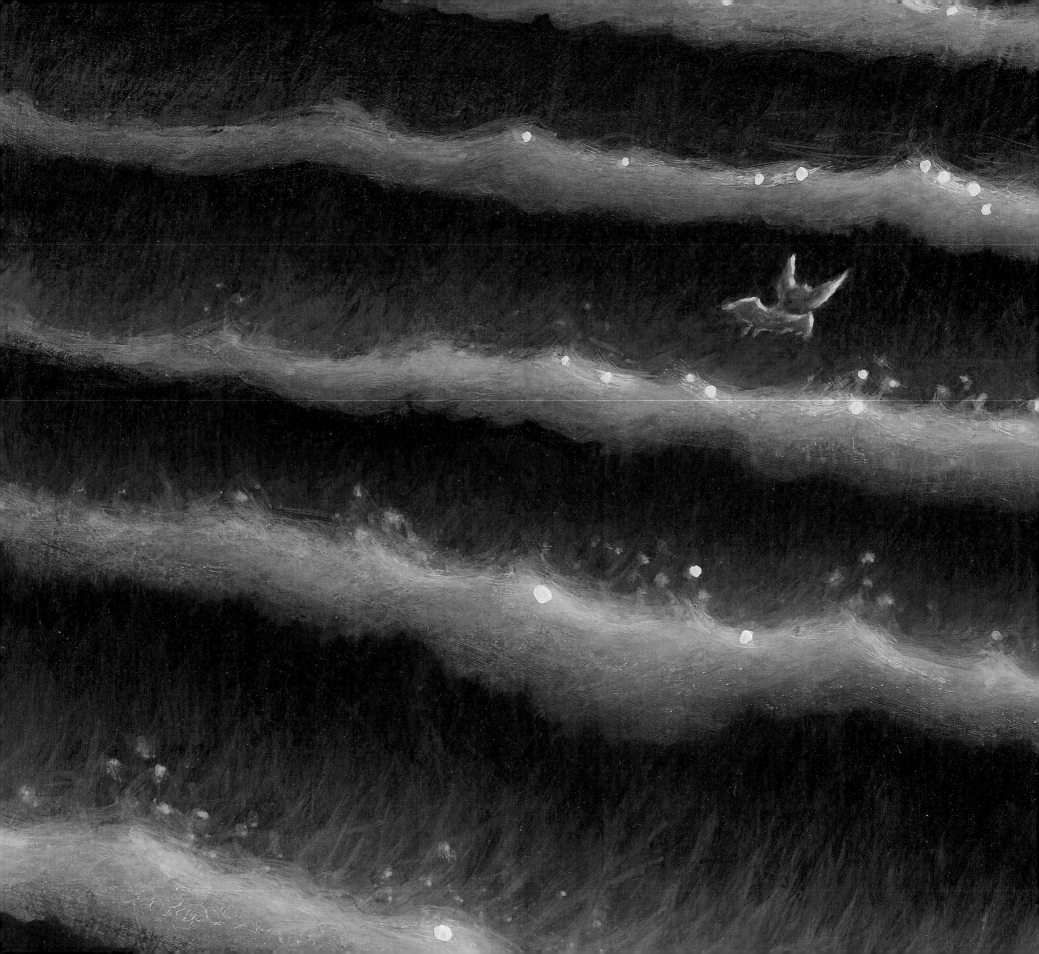

Out went his song over dark water then, again and again, each wave on the ocean rising up to greet him, each splash of sea foam becoming kin to him.

The sky began to change, grow light, and cast long shadows over the shore. With the morning came memory: his mother's voice, her warm wings. Chiro knew it was time to go home.

Flying higher than he'd ever flown, Chiro began to sing, listening, listening . . .

The music of the land rose up in all of its many textures, each tree, each cliff, each place he'd passed, until finally the song of home added its voice to the others.

His cave called out from the blanketing shrubs and pillows of moss at its mouth, and Chiro followed that familiar sound back into the sheltering earth.

His mother caught him all up in her wings and asked, "Was it very dark in the world, Little Wing? What did you see?"

"Why, Momma!" Chiro said laughing, "It was very, VERY dark . . .

. . . and I saw everything!"

And then he yawned and turned his head into the
warmth of her body, letting the rising sun's quiet song
carry him, lull him, sing him to sleep.

The name Chiro (*cheer-o*) was inspired by the word "chiroptera," (from Greek, *cheir,* "hand" and *pteron,* "wing"), the order name for bats, the only mammals capable of true flight.